D0592465

READER COLLECTION

LEGO Friends

We Stick Together!

No part of this publication may be reproduced, stored in a retrieval system, or transmitted in any form or by any means, electronic, mechanical, photocopying, recording, or otherwise, without written permission of the publisher. For information regarding permission, write to Scholastic Inc., Attention: Permissions Department, 557 Broadway, New York, NY 10012.

LEGO® Friends: A Puppy Tale (978-0-545-51754-6) © 2013 The LEGO Group.
LEGO® Friends: Andrea Takes the Stage (978-0-545-51756-0) © 2013 The LEGO Group.
LEGO® Friends: Double Trouble (978-0-545-56667-4) © 2014 The LEGO Group.
LEGO® Friends: Meet the Friends (978-0-545-59943-6) © 2013 The LEGO Group.

ISBN 978-1-4351-5838-2

LEGO, the LEGO logo and the Brick and Knob configurations are trademarks and/or copyrights of the LEGO Group. © 2014 The LEGO Group. Produced by Scholastic Inc. under license from the LEGO Group.

Published by Scholastic Inc. SCHOLASTIC and associated logos are trademarks and/or registered trademarks of Scholastic Inc.

12 11 10 9 8 7 6 5 4 3 16 17 18 19 20/0

Printed in China 38

This edition first printing, October 2014

SCHOLASTIC INC.

LEGO
Friends
A Puppy Tale
SCHOLASTIC

It was a beautiful day in Heartlake City. Mia was taking her puppy, Charlie, to the vet.
Come on, Charlie! It's time for your checkup.
Woof!

Andrea was leaving the City Park Café when she spotted Mia.
Hi, Mia! Are you taking Charlie to the vet?
He doesn't look very happy. Wait, I know! Stay right here!
AROOOO!

Andrea went into the café and came back with some homemade dog biscuits.
If you're a good boy at the vet, Charlie, you can have some treats!
Woof! Woof!

Soon, the girls reached the Heartlake City Vet. Olivia was there giving animals checkups.
Hi, Olivia!
We're here for Charlie's checkup.
Great! Come on in.

Olivia began Charlie's exam.
His heart sounds strong!
BA-BUMP! BA-BUMP!
Let's see how much you weigh. You gained half a pound!
Arf!

Andrea gave Charlie a treat.
You're doing great, Charlie!
Now we have to take some X-rays.
Bow-wow.
Don't worry, Charlie. This won't hurt a bit.

Charlie thought the X-ray machine was big and scary.
And he ran out the door!
Charlie, no!
Woof! Woof! Aroooo!

Mia chased Charlie down the street . . .
Charlie, *come back!*

. . . but the puppy was too fast for her.
Whew—I—*gasp*—can't run another step!
Don't worry, Mia. We'll help track him down.

Just then, Stephanie drove by.
Hi, girls. What's going on?
My puppy, Charlie, is missing.
We were at the vet when Charlie got scared and ran off.
He went that way!
We tried to chase him, but he was too fast.

I'll help you find him. Hop in!
VROOOMM!

The girls drove all over Heartlake City. But they couldn't spot Charlie anywhere.
Just then . . .
Wait, look over there. Charlie's collar!

Well, now we know Charlie was here. But which way did he go?
Hmm. Are there any other clues we could follow?

Hey! There's a trail of crumbs!
What do crumbs have to do with Charlie?
I gave Charlie a treat at the vet's office.
I see! If we follow the crumbs, we'll find Charlie!

The girls followed the trail through the park.
Here, boy!
Charlie!
Oh, Charlie!
Where could he be?

The crumbs led the girls to Ambersands Beach.
It's so crowded. We'll never find him.
Look! There're Emma and Jacob. Maybe they saw Charlie.

Hi, guys! Have either of you seen Charlie? We think he ran this way.
No, sorry.
I haven't seen him, either.
Jacob, I think you can help us find Charlie.

Me?
Yes, you! Is anyone using the sea plane?
Oh! You want Jacob to fly over the beach and look for Charlie!
You'll be able to spot him from above.
Great idea! But I'll need a copilot. Stephanie, are you ready to fly?
Aye, aye, Captain!

Soon, Jacob and Stephanie were soaring high above Ambersands Beach.

See anything?
Yes! Over there! I see paw prints.
Jacob made a tight turn.
Hang on! I'm going closer.

Okay back there?
Sure, doing fine!
Here we go!
Wahooooo!

The plane flew closer to the beach.
Come in, Olivia. We spotted some paw prints near the shoreline.
Copy that, Jacob.

Jacob says they saw some paw prints that way.
Let's go!
Right there! I see them.
There he is! CHARLIE!

I'm so glad we found you!
Woof! Woof!
You sure gave us a scare.

Jacob and Stephanie spotted the friends below.
They found Charlie!
Yeah!

Stephanie helped Jacob land the plane.

Thanks so much for your help, Jacob!
That was great teamwork.
No problem!

We couldn't have done it without you—and one another. Right, girls?
Right!

I'd better get the plane back to the flight school. See you all later!
Bye, Jacob!
Thanks again!

Charlie can play for bit before we go back to the vet.
I think that's a great idea. It'll calm him down.
Arf!
How about some ice cream to celebrate?

The girls spent the rest of the afternoon at the beach.
Hey Charlie, want to play fetch?
I think he's saying, "yes."
Just promise you'll come *right back*!
Arooooo!

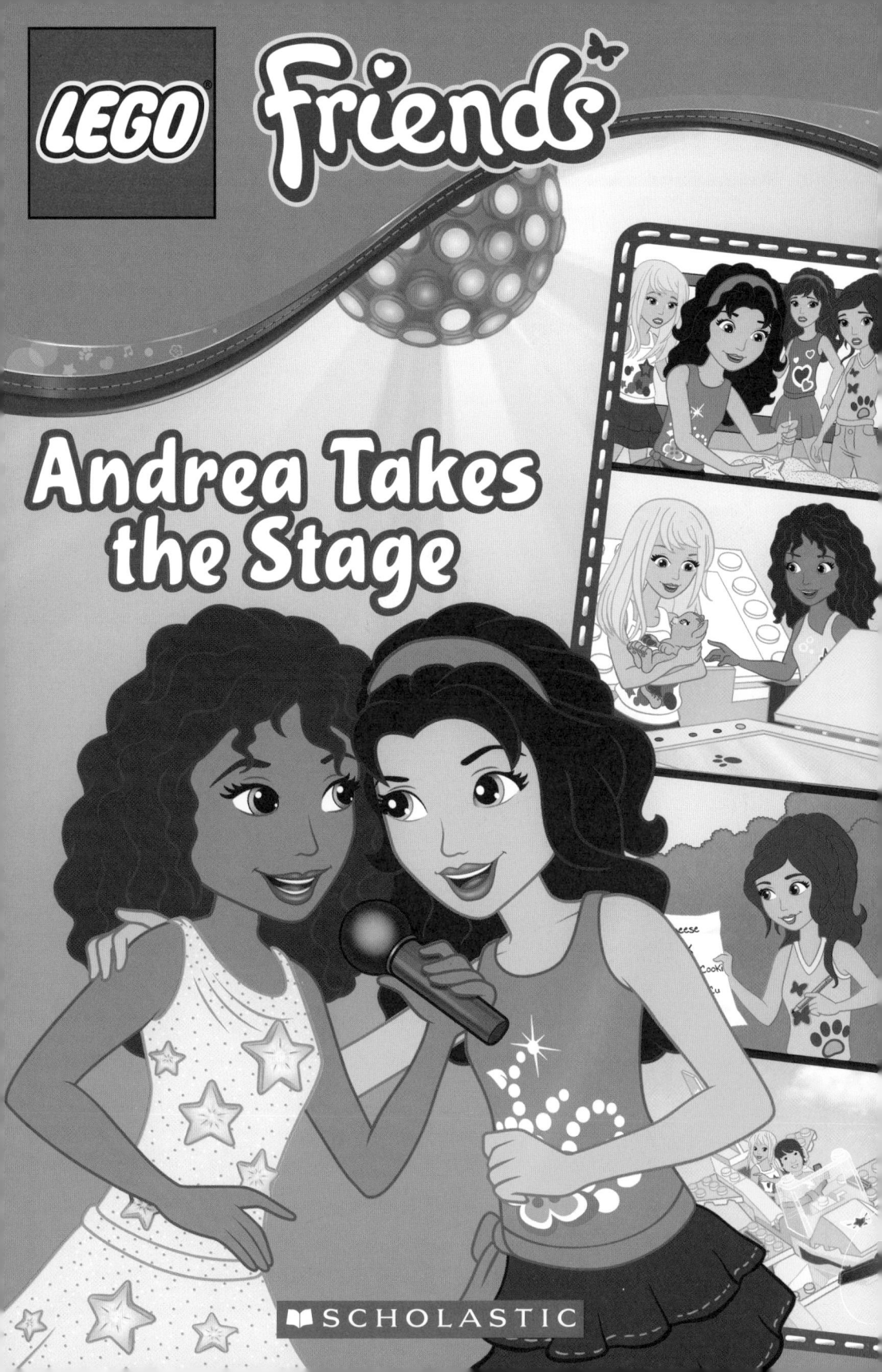
LEGO
Friends
Andrea Takes the Stage
SCHOLASTIC

Mia, Stephanie, Olivia, and Emma came to see Andrea at the City Park Café.
My new song is ready!
Let's hear it!

Wait! I have a better idea. Let's throw a party here, and you can sing it then!
That sounds like a lot of work. . . .
Not if we all help. I can make the invitations.
And I can order the food.

I know just the design for your dress.
And I have a great idea for the stage, if you all help me build it.
You bet!
Café
Thanks, guys. This will be fun!

The friends each got to work. Stephanie and Andrea made invitations.
This looks perfect!
Meow!
CONCERT
CITY PARK
CAFÉ
7:00 PM
FRIDAY
Oops! Maxie, you stepped in the paint.
We'd better wash your paws.

With Maxie all cleaned up, Stephanie copied the invitations.
Purrrr.
BEEP! BEEP!
Then the girls drove all over Heartlake City to deliver them.

Later, Andrea met Mia at the bakery.
It looks like Charlie wants to help us pick food for the party!
Woof! Woof!
Yummy!
It's going to be hard to choose. It's all so good!
Munch! Munch!

Mia wrote down the food order. But Charlie kept distracting her.
Oh, Charlie.
Arf! Arf!
Cheese
Milk
Sugar Cooki
Fruit Cu
Andrea tried to keep Charlie quiet.
Here, Charlie! Fetch!
Woof! Woof!

Meanwhile, Emma finished designing Andrea's dress.
Now, where's that sparkly fabric gone to, Prince?
Ribbit! Ribbit!

After Emma found the fabric, she started sewing.
This is going to be beautiful on Andrea!
BOING! BOING!
Later, Andrea tried on the dress.
It's *so* you!
Thanks, Emma. I love it!

Olivia had the plans for the stage done in no time at all.
What do you think, Goldie?
Tweet! Tweet!
The girls headed to the City Park Café.
Café
Let's start building!
We're ready to roll!

They lifted bricks and hammered away.
Just a little to the left and it will be perfect.
You got it.

Just then, Jacob stopped by. He wanted to see the show. But something was wrong.
I can't read what time the show starts.
Oh, no! Maxie's paw print was accidentally copied onto the invitations!
CONCERT
CITY PARK
CAFÉ
00 PM
FRIDAY
How can we let people know the right time?

Come on, Jacob. We need to head to the skies!
CONCERT CITY PARK CAFÉ 7:00 PM FRIDAY
Soon, everyone in town knew the right time!

The next day, the girls met up at the café for the food delivery.
I hope we got enough.
It smells yummy!

But the food order was all wrong.
It's only ingredients.
I didn't think we had to cook.
FLOUR
SUGAR
MILK
Charlie was distracting me. I must have written the order wrong.

But it's okay. With this kitchen, we can cook anything!
Is there enough time?
FLOUR
SUGAR
There will be if we work together!

The friends chopped, mixed, baked, and decorated.
How about star cakes, star cookies, and star fruit?
That sounds stellar!
We did it!

With one more mess avoided, Andrea put on her dress.
Testing, one, two, three . . .
You look *and* sound great!

Suddenly, the power went out!
BZZZZT! BZZZZT!
We can't have a show without lights and sound.
It's an easy fix . . . if I can find the fuse box.

Andrea held up some glow sticks.
I know where the fuse box is.
Lead the way!
Whew! I'm so glad you knew where to look!
It's right over here.

Olivia got to work on the fuse box.
Just a few more switches and we'll be all set.

The lights came back on!
You did it, Olivia!
But Andrea's dress was torn!
I must have snagged it when we were in the dark.
Oh, no, Andrea. Your dress!

How will you perform now?
It's okay. I can sing in my normal clothes. After all the hard work you guys have done, the show must go on!

Wait! With my sewing kit, I can fix anything. I just need a bit of star power.
How about these?
I can make that work!

Emma quickly sewed pieces of star fruit onto the dress.
Almost done!
Hurry, Emma—the show's about to start!

Wow, Andrea.
It's so beautiful! Thank you, Emma!
You look gorgeous!

Thanks to her friends' help, Andrea was ready to take the stage.
My new song goes out to my friends, who made this party happen.

No matter what we do, I can count on you . . .
Go, Andrea!
The crowd went wild!

After the show, the friends joined Andrea on stage.
That was amazing!
I couldn't have done it without you guys.

You were already a star on the inside.
So it wasn't hard to make you shine!

LEGO
Friends
Double Trouble
SCHOLASTIC

One day at Heartlake High . . .
CLUB FAIR TODAY!
Wow! This activity fair is awesome.
There are so many clubs.
I can't decide which one to join.

It looks like Andrea already has.
Hey, girls! I just joined the Heartlake High Chorus.
This is the song director, Mrs. Lee.
We're excited to have Andrea sing with us. Our first concert is next Friday.
Wow! That's great!

In fact, we have a favor to ask you girls.
We need people to work on costumes, lights, and sound.
costumes
lights
sound
You had me at "costumes!"
We're in!
Thanks, girls! We couldn't do it without you.

Stephanie joined her friends as they walked to class.
Guess what, guys. I joined the soccer team. The coach is making me a forward!
Wow—that's amazing, Stephanie!

Thanks! But I'm really nervous. I'm the youngest player on the team. Will you guys come to my first game?
Of course!
We can't wait to cheer you on.
Olivia
You guys are the best! See you later!

After Stephanie left, Andrea noticed something.
Come See the Soccer Team's First Game Next Friday!
Oh, no!
Come See the Soccer Team's First Game Next Friday!
My concert and Stephanie's soccer game are on the same night!

Yikes! What are we going to do?
Let's talk to Mrs. Lee. Maybe only one of us needs to work the concert.
I'm sorry, girls. It's definitely a three-person job. I'm counting on you.
Is it okay if only one of us works the show?
Now what?
We'll have to tell Stephanie. Maybe she'll understand.

Later, Olivia and Mia went to the soccer field.
Hey, Stephanie! Can we talk to you?
Sure! But first, watch this.
Dribbbble
Score!
As long as you guys are here, I'll play just like that next Friday!

That's just it, Steph. We—
Can't wait to see you play! Right, Mia? We have to run— bye!
Why didn't you tell her? We can't be in two places at once.
I know, but she was so excited. We'll figure something out.

The next day, at Science Club . . .
Hi, Olivia.
Oh, hi, Jacob.
I'm fixing these walkie-talkies. They work in places cell phones can't.
Oh . . . cool.
Is something wrong?
Stephanie wants us at her game next Friday. But we promised to work Andrea's concert that night.

Olivia and Jacob test the walkie-talkies.
Stephanie must be pretty bummed.
We haven't told her yet.
You haven't? Why not?
She was so excited. I didn't want to disappoint her.
Won't she be more hurt if you can't come and you didn't tell her?
I guess you're right.

Later, the girls did homework together.
Stephanie, we need to tell you something.
What's up?
We can't come to your game.
But why? You promised!
We already signed up to work Andrea's concert.
You're going to Andrea's concert, but not my game?

We didn't know they were the same night. We're so sorry, Steph.
I can't believe you guys won't be there. I-I've got to go.
I feel terrible.
This is all my fault. I shouldn't have asked you guys to help with my concert.

You didn't know. If only there was a way to see Stephanie's game at the same time.
HIGH SCHOOL
Wait a minute. What about our smartphones? Olivia, do you think Jacob would stream us video of Stephanie's game?
That's a great idea! Let's go ask him.

At the auditorium . . .
I'd love to help, girls, but there's no cell service in here.
I guess there really *isn't* anything we can do.
Don't be so sure.
Jacob, can you think of anything that works where cell phones can't?
Olivia, you're a genius!

The following Friday, at the concert . . .
Thank you so much, guys. I really appreciate your help!
Anytime! And, Olivia, is your plan ready?
Just about. Jacob? Come in, Jacob. Can you hear me?

Over on the soccer field . . .
Do you read me, Jacob?
Loud and clear, Olivia!
How are you doing, Stephanie?
I'm really nervous. I wish the others were here, too.
Just wait. I think they might surprise you.

The concert and soccer game were both about to begin.
All right, Jacob. Here we go!
Everything's ready, Olivia!

Here's to our dear
Heartlake High...
All that practice really paid off. The chorus sounds amazing!

During the intermission, the girls focused on the soccer game.
Stephanie's shooting for the goal. Oh, she just missed!
Come on, Stephanie. We know you can do it!

Back on the field . . .
Good try, Stephanie!
Thanks, Jacob. But I'm not doing very well.
That's not true. We know you're doing great!
Olivia? Emma? Mia? Is that you?

I think Stephanie's figured out the surprise.
We're here for you, Stephanie!
You guys did this for me? You're the best! Now watch—I mean, *listen* to this!
Stephanie stole the ball from the other team!
You can do it, Stephanie! Go for the goal!

Just then, the concert intermission ended.
It's almost time for Andrea's solo, Jacob. But we'll have the walkie-talkie right here.
Sounds good. I'll keep you posted on Steph's game!

The friends watched Andrea sing her solo onstage.
We can do it, if you just believe!
Her voice is magical!

A short while later . . .
Brava, Andrea! That was an amazing concert.
Guys, is it finished? Hurry over here! The game is going into overtime!
We can still make it!
Let's go!

We're coming, Stephanie!
Jacob, we're on our way!
All right!
The girls arrived at the field just in time.
Did we make it? Is it over?
Nope. Look— there goes Stephanie!

She's got the ball.
2:2
2:2
And there's only a minute left!
Kick!
Hurray!
Goal for Heartlake High!

I can't believe you guys heard the whole game!
Jacob gave us an awesome play-by-play. It was like we were right here on the sidelines.

It was all thanks to Olivia's idea.
We knew how much it meant to you.

Thank you so much. I don't know what I'd do without you guys.
That goes double for me!

LEGO
Friends
Fun facts, quizzes, and more!
Meet the Friends
SCHOLASTIC

Welcome to Heartlake City

Meet Andrea, Mia, Emma, Olivia, and Stephanie. They're five best friends with unique personalities, and when they come together, they make the perfect team! Turn the page to learn fun facts about each girl, and then take the different quizzes to find out what makes your group of friends special.

Meet the Friends

Mia

Whether she's putting on a magic show or running in the school track meet, Mia loves being active. She enjoys playing all kinds of sports and practicing magic tricks to impress her friends. But if there's one thing Mia adores more than anything, it's animals. She's terrific with pets and even has her own horse, Bella.

While everyone has just five senses, Emma's friends swear that she has a sixth: fashion sense. With just a glance, Emma knows exactly how to make an outfit more glamorous, a room more colorful, or a painting more beautiful! She keeps her friends looking stylish, even when they're just hanging out in Olivia's tree house.

Emma

Andrea is a very talented singer, and she dreams of being a star someday! Whether she's rehearsing a new song or serving muffins at the café, she is always full of energy. Her friends say that she can be a bit dramatic sometimes, but what's life without a little excitement?

Olivia

If there's a computer that needs fixing or an invention to be tinkered with, Olivia is the girl for the job. She can design and build almost anything—even a mini robot! She's also one of the funniest girls in Heartlake City. Her jokes always have the friends rolling with laughter.

Stephanie is outgoing and friendly, and loves working on group projects. When she's not hanging out, she's sure to be organizing something. Stephanie always has her notebook nearby to write down the week's schedule and make sure everything runs according to plan.

Stephanie

Heartlake City

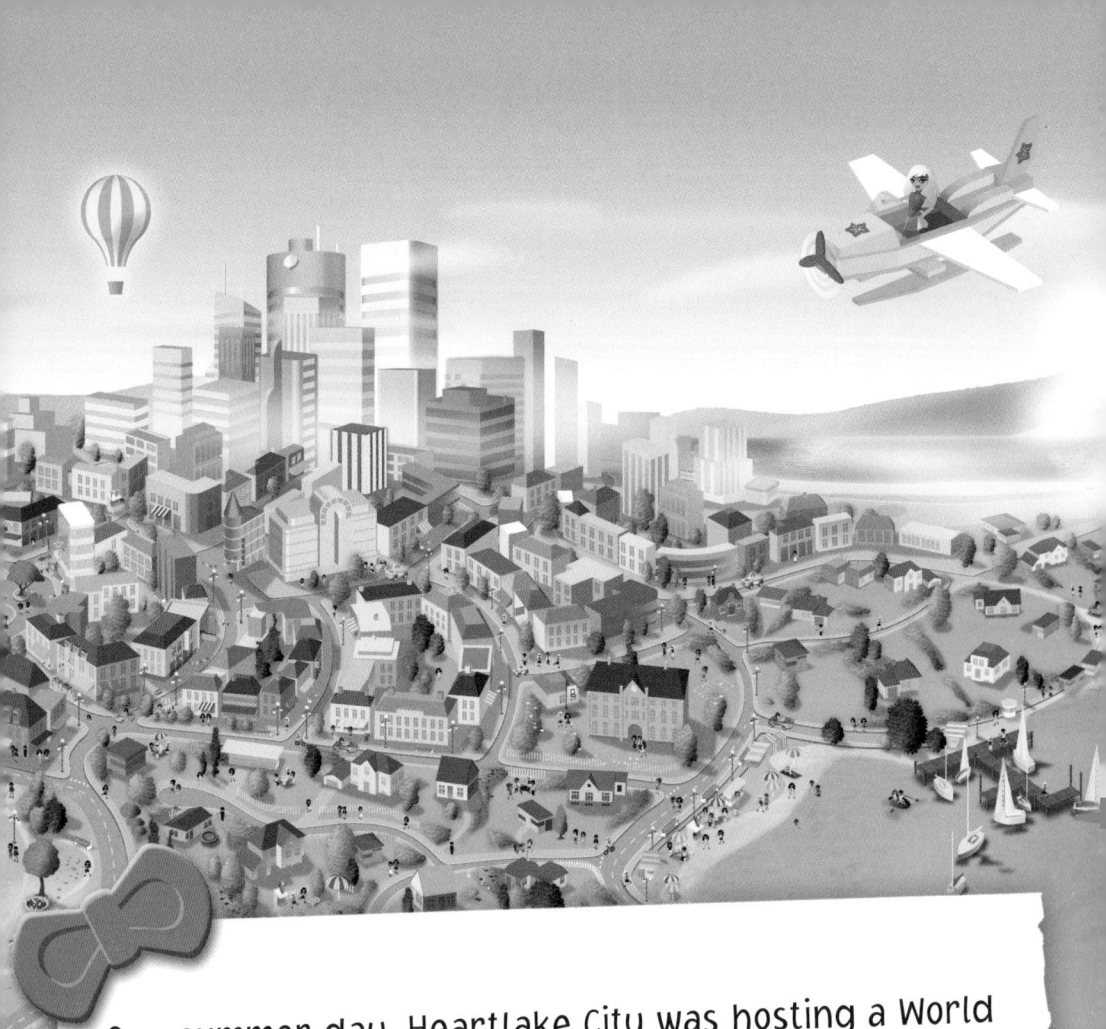

One summer day, Heartlake City was hosting a World Petacular celebration. Mia, Andrea, Stephanie, Emma, and Olivia met there by accident, and they've been inseparable ever since! The five girls are all in the same grade at Heartlake High, so they're always working together on homework, planning school events, or heading to sports games. Most weekends they hang out at the City Park Café. But if they're not there, you'll be sure to find them up in Olivia's tree house, sharing stories and secrets.

Perfect Pets

Each of the friends has her very own pet that matches her personality purr-fectly! Read about their cute animals, and then decide which pet would be your perfect companion.

Charlie

Charlie is Mia's very curious—and very hungry—puppy. Mia spends hours playing fetch with him in the park. When she doesn't have her eye on him, he often gets into mischief by chasing butterflies or sneaking treats from picnic baskets.

Kitty

Stephanie's white cat, Kitty, adores naps in the sunshine or chasing balls of yarn. Whenever Stephanie feels stressed about event planning, Kitty is there with an extra nuzzle. It doesn't hurt that Stephanie usually has a treat or two on hand as well!

Sunshine

Emma was nervous about learning to ride horses at the Heartlake Stables. But all that changed when she met Sunshine. Gentle and patient, Sunshine was cantering with Emma in no time. And Emma enjoys brushing Sunshine's silky mane.

Oscar

Oscar the hedgehog's prickly nature is the perfect match for Andrea's spunky personality. He's not the cuddliest pet in the world, but he likes listening to Andrea's new song lyrics. And Andrea makes sure to give him lots of attention, too.

Maxie

When Olivia first moved to Heartlake City, it took her a little while to make friends. Until she did, Maxie helped her feel right at home. This sweet kitten loves to explore and climb on new things. Olivia quickly created plenty of inventive cat toys to keep Maxie busy!

Which pet would match your personality best?

Stephanie

About Me

Quote: "Everything's under control . . . almost!"

Favorite activities: Party planning and writing

Favorite books: Fantasy novels

Someday I want to be: An author

What my friends say about me: "We trust Stephanie to keep us on time . . . and keep a secret!"

Best Memory

One time, a new book from my favorite author was about to go on sale. I'd been looking forward to buying it for weeks! I even helped the store plan a book party to celebrate. Little did I know, my friends planned a surprise, too. They invited the author to my party, and she signed my copy! It was the best night ever.

Secret Tricks

When Mia performed a magic show in the school talent festival, I was her assistant. She swore me to secrecy about her card tricks. To this day, I haven't told anyone how she did them. I wanted her to know she could trust me. When someone asks me about them, I just say, "It was magic!"

Quiz: Can You Be Trusted?

Take this quiz to find out if you're a trustworthy friend like Stephanie!

Your friend tells you a secret. What do you do?

A I'd only tell my close friends. But I'd swear them to secrecy, too.

B I would never tell anyone. My friend can trust me.

C If it was really a secret, then my friend would never have shared it. So it's okay to spill.

My friends:

A tell me simply everything about themselves!

B ask me for advice with tough problems.

C know it's sometimes difficult for me to hold my tongue.

If I make a promise to a friend:

A I try to stick to it. But I make so many promises, it's hard to keep track!

B I always come through, even if I have to cancel other plans.

C I intend to keep it, but sometimes forget.

I have:

A loads of friends, and we talk about everything. And everyone.

B a small group of close friends.

C many people I hang out with but don't consider "true" friends.

Now count which answer you have chosen the most and see if people can trust you.

Mostly As: You're very outgoing and friendly, and a bit of a social butterfly. However, you sometimes reveal too much or make promises you can't keep.

GOOD ADVICE: If your friend tells you a secret, remember that she trusts you to keep it. And maybe only make a few promises, rather than a lot. That way, you can follow through on the ones that count.

Mostly Bs: You are the queen of keeping quiet. When somebody tells you a secret, your lips are zipped. You always keep your promises, and you expect others to do the same.

GOOD ADVICE: Don't stress too much about being the keeper of everyone's secrets. Sometimes, you have to give yourself a break, too!

Mostly Cs: Many people are always around because you have juicy gossip to share. But spilling secrets makes it hard for others to trust you.

GOOD ADVICE: Being popular by spreading interesting news isn't the same as having close friends. Try sticking with a small group of friends and sharing fewer secrets. Your friendships will be much stronger!

Mia

About Me

Quote: "Let's get to work!"

Favorite activities: Horseback riding, magic tricks

Favorite books: Stories about animals

Someday I want to be: A veterinarian

What my friends say about me: "Sometimes we think Mia might like animals more than people."

Going for Gold

This is my horse, Bella. We enter lots of riding competitions together. Another rider named Lacy and her horse, Gingersnap, are our main competitors. We don't always win, but I know I can count on Bella to do her best!

If I Were Writing a Story . . .

I'd probably write an adventure about animals living in a magical world . . . where they could talk! My dog, Charlie, barks when he's hungry, and Bella nuzzles me when she wants attention. But I'd love to really be able to talk to animals. Imagine all the cool things they'd have to say!

Quiz: What's Your Perfect Pet?

If you could have any pet, what would it be? Take this quiz to find out which animal resembles you the most!

I prefer...
- a teddy bear → **My favorite drink is...**
- a photo album → **I will do homework...**

My favorite drink is...
- fruit juice → **I enjoy vacationing...**
- warm cocoa → **I like to relax...**

I will do homework...
- with music on → **I like to relax...**
- in silence → **For a big party, I'll wear...**

I enjoy vacationing...
- at the beach → **I prefer...**
- in the city → **When I'm at home...**

I like to relax...
- in the park → **When I'm at home...**
- on the sofa → **My favorite jewelry is...**

For a big party, I'll wear...
- velvet → **My favorite jewelry is...**
- sequins → **I like to travel...**

I prefer...
- freedom → **A horse**
- schedules → **A dog**

When I'm at home...
- I feel very comfortable → **A dog**
- I always want to go out → **A cat**

My favorite jewelry is...
- silver → **A canary**
- gold → **A canary**

I like to travel...
- by plane → **A canary**
- by ship → **A fish**

A Horse

You're fond of nature, just like Mia. You dislike too many rules and can sometimes be a bit bossy. So your ideal animal is a horse. Together you would gallop off into the sunset. Maybe it's time for you to visit the nearest stable?

A Dog

You are hardworking and loyal, just like Stephanie. You spend your free time doing outdoor activities, but you also like for things to be on schedule. The perfect pet for you is a dog! Together you can spend hours playing outside and taking walks.

A Cat

You enjoy freedom and doing things on your own, but you also like knowing you can count on close friends for support. Just like Olivia, the perfect pet for you is a cat—this animal may seem to be a loner, but it also likes to be cuddled and stroked.

A Bird

Music fills almost every part of your life. This makes you very similar to Andrea, and your perfect pet should love music as much as you! Your best choice would be a bird who will sing sweet tunes. Who knows? Maybe one day you will perform a duet.

A Fish

Though you like animals, you're not exactly a "pet person." You enjoy designing cute pet outfits more than actually playing a game of fetch. The perfect choice for you would be a fish. You could admire its colors and decorate its tank with accessories!

Olivia

About Me

Quote: "It's easy! Or at least, we can figure it out."

Favorite activities: Inventions, photography

Favorite books: Textbooks

Someday I want to be: A scientist

What my friends say about me: "We count on Olivia for awesome inventions . . . and help with our homework."

My Tree House

One of my favorite spots is the tree house in my backyard. My friends come over to hang out here, eat snacks, and share stories. One time, we had a sleepover all weekend. My parents brought us up food and blankets so we could stay in the tree house all night.

Funniest Story

Last year, we were assigned a school science project to come up with a new invention. My friends couldn't believe it when I designed a vacuum cleaner that played music! But when the vacuum was on, you couldn't hear the song. So it was back to the drawing board.

Quiz: Friendship Test

The five friends know they can have fun together and rely on one another whenever they need a helping hand. Are you a reliable friend? Take this quiz to find out!

What do you do when:

Your friend is sick. Do you:

- Visit her and cheer her up. ✶✶✶
- Tell her about the good times you're having with your other friends. ✶
- Take notes in class for her so she doesn't fall behind. ✶✶

You only have one chocolate bar, and your friend sits down next to you. Do you:

- Give it to your friend. You don't really like chocolate, anyway. ✶✶
- Quickly eat it! ✶
- Divide it in half and share it with your friend. ✶✶✶

Your friend wants to perform in the school karaoke contest, but she's not a great singer. Do you:

- Give her some pointers. ✶✶
- Sing with her. It'll be fun if you're together! ✶✶✶
- Laugh when she can't hit all the notes. ✶

Your friend is taking part in the same race as you. Do you:

- Let her think she's winning. Then cut in front of her right at the finish line. ✶
- Let her win. ✶✶
- Enjoy the race and cheer her on, no matter which one of you wins. ✶✶✶

When your friend tells you her biggest secret, do you:

- Tell her a secret in return. ✶✶
- Let her know her secret is safe with you. ✶✶✶
- Tell your other friends the moment she's gone! ✶

From 5 to 7 ✶

Hmm . . . friendship is not your strongest point. But it's something you can work on! The next time you're with your friend, try to put her needs ahead of your own. And pay a bit more attention to her feelings. You'll be a great friend in no time!

From 8 to 11 ✶

You are very helpful, and everyone likes being around you. You take care of your friend and do everything for her. However, don't forget to think about yourself sometimes, too. Friendship is about being happy together!

From 12 to 15 ✶

Having you as a friend is like winning the jackpot. You are a very reliable person, and you are always there for your friend—no matter what. You share everything together, and your friendship makes you both stronger.

Emma

About Me

Quote: "That is so you!"

Favorite activities: Drawing, sewing

Favorite books: Fashion magazines

Someday I want to be: A costume designer

What my friends say about me: "Emma, come quick. We need a makeover!"

Picture-Perfect

My friends and I were helping out at a kindergarten art camp one summer. The campers wanted to draw our pictures, so we fixed our hair and posed while they colored. We thought we looked pretty cool, but the drawings turned out different than we expected! My friends and I still laugh every time we look at them.

Emma's Fashion Tips

It's fun showcasing your personality with fashion. I always tell my friends, just take a little extra time in the morning to do something special. Try a new hairstyle. Wear a colorful belt or bracelet. Even paint your fingernails. Fashion is about expressing yourself.

Quiz: What's Your Personality?

Take this quiz with your friends to find out what roles you play in your group.

In the shopping mall:

A I always have a shopping list.
B I can't wait to leave.
C I rush to the bookstore.
D I hang out at the coffee shop.
E I help my friends carry their bags.

The accessory that suits me best is:

A A digital watch
B A tool kit
C A camera
D A colorful MP3 player
E A glittery lip balm

In a school performance:

A I'm the director.
B I design the set.
C I run the sound board.
D I play the leading role.
E I make the costumes.

The perfect symbol to describe me would be:

A ★ B 🦋 C ♥ D ♫ E ☘

Now count which answer you have chosen most often and see which role you play in your group of friends!

Mostly As:

A Master of Organization:

If there's a party to be planned or a meeting to be held, you're there one minute early with a list of things to do. Just remember to have fun while you're doing all that scheduling.

Mostly Bs:

A Handy Girl: You are the go-to girl everyone relies on when something needs to be moved, built, or repaired. Your friends appreciate your help—and admire how handy you are.

Mostly Cs:

A Thinker: Complicated calculations? A new invention? You can't wait to get started! You are very smart and are always thinking of ways to improve things—or reinvent them!

Mostly Ds:

A Star: Do you sing along with every song on the radio? Are you the first in line for musical tryouts? You were born to perform! Thanks to your outgoing personality, you make friends easily and make their lives more colorful.

Mostly Es:

A Fashionista: You enjoy tasks the most when they require artistic expertise. Your outfits look perfect each day, you always know which colors go best together, and your friends come to you for makeovers.

Andrea

About Me

Quote: "Music puts life in full color!"

Favorite activities: Singing, acting

Favorite books: Movie scripts

Someday I want to be: An actress or musician

What my friends say about me: "We've already asked Andrea for her autograph because we know she'll be a star someday!"

Most Embarrassing Moment

Our school was holding auditions for a new musical. I couldn't wait to try out! I practiced my audition for weeks. But on the big night, I accidently went to the wrong classroom. A debate tournament was going on, and I didn't realize it. When I sang to the audience, they were completely confused!

Rock Star

Check out these new song lyrics I wrote about my friends. Can you think of a pretty melody to sing it to? Let's sing it together!

No matter where I am, on sea or land,
my friends are there to lend a hand.
Together we can do anything,
as long as there are songs to sing!

Quiz: It's Showtime!

Take this quiz with your friends to see what type of movie you should each star in.

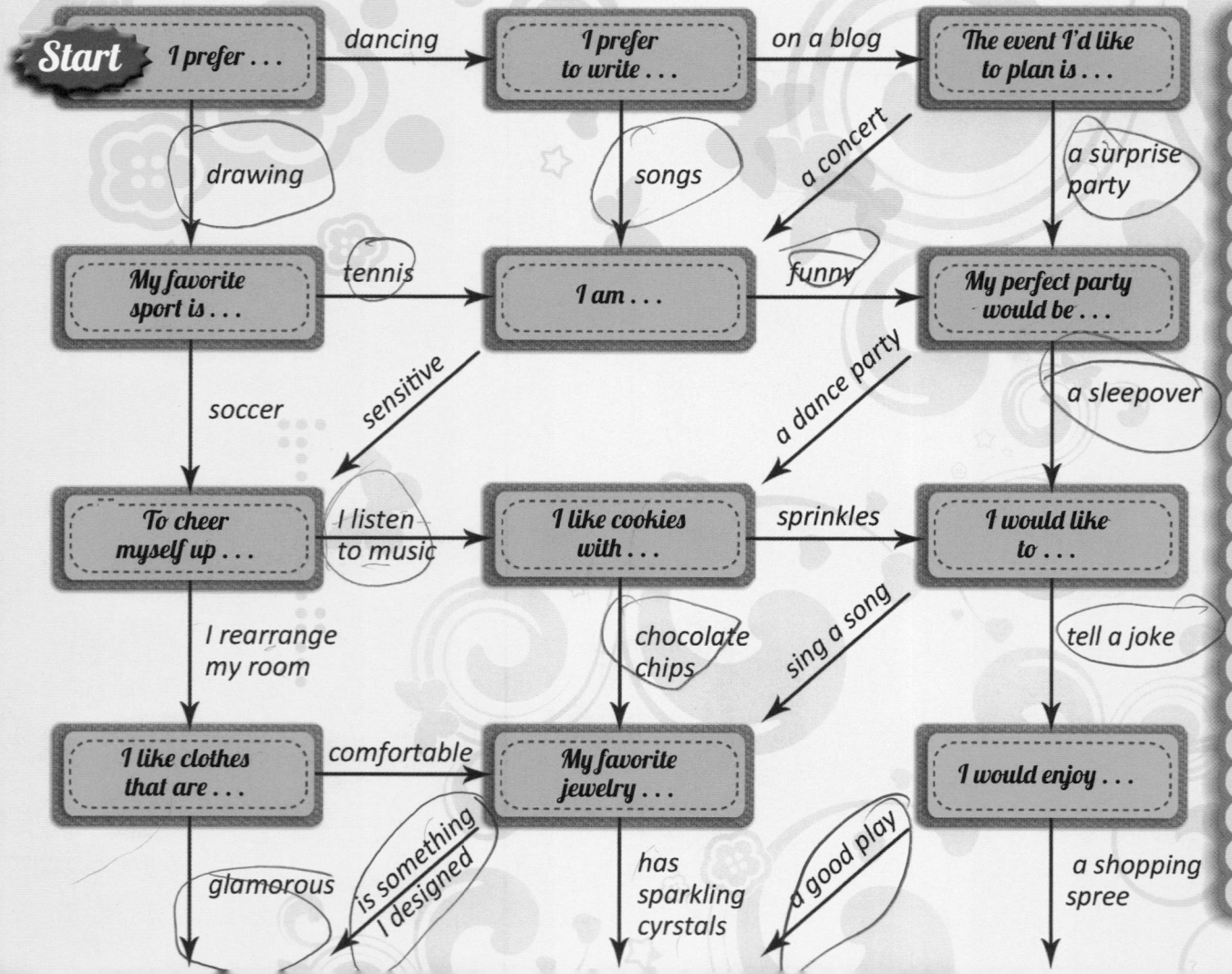